Dedication:

to my first born daughter,
whose determination is an
inspiration to all of us.

Table of Contents

Chapter One

The Right Ingredients

1

Cooking Sunday dinner with Dad was a ritual at Katie's house. It was the day of the week that Katie loved most. Daddy would ask, "Who wants to help me cook dinner tonight?"

Katie was always the first one in her family to say, "I do."

Katie was seven years old when she began volunteering to help her dad prepare meals. She loved to cook.

The first thing Dad and Katie did was pull the step stool up to the kitchen counter, put on aprons and, of course, their "Kiss the Cook" hats. Now, they both looked like real chefs.

Katie and her dad would browse through their collection of cookbooks and decide what they were going to prepare. It was always a gourmet meal. When they found their recipe they opened the cookbook and laid it on the counter. They pulled the ingredients out of the pantry to ensure they had everything they needed for their recipe.

Sometimes they had to drive to the grocery store to buy an ingredient they did not have at home. Once they returned home they would announce to the family what they were preparing.

"Tonight, we will be serving Oysters Rockefeller," Katie proudly proclaimed. This was her favorite appetizer.

"Yuck," was her sister and two brothers' response.

"The production begins," said Dad. Katie and her Dad laid newspapers on the counter, because cooking oysters is a very messy job. They used a kitchen tool called an oyster shucker.

They opened all the oysters with the shucker and laid the shells on the newspapers. They scooped the oysters out of the shells with spoons and rinsed them off with water.

The next step was making the toppings. They cooked the bacon just perfectly and rinsed the spinach. Katie and her dad chopped and mixed all the ingredients together. The oysters were then ready to be topped and baked.

The process took a long time, but Katie and her Dad loved creating meals together. The time they spent together was very special for both of them.

Katie's next job was to set the table for their fancy meal. Katie placed a tablecloth on the table and used their pretty cloth napkins.

When the table was set and the preparations complete, Katie said, "Mom, the Katie and Daddy restaurant is now open."

Mom was their best customer. She happily ate the oysters and complimented the chefs, "These are the finest oysters I have ever tasted! Thank you for making dinner for us tonight."

Naturally, the kitchen was a total disaster when they finished cooking. Katie's least favorite part of cooking was cleaning up the kitchen when she was done.

Mom said, "Cleaning up is also a big part of cooking."

Katie thought the oysters tasted great, so the mess was worth it.

CHAPTER TWO

Katie's Cafe

2

As Katie grew older she cooked all the time. In the morning, she would ask her Mom, "Can I make macaroni and cheese for lunch today?" She learned how to make it perfectly. She also learned how to be safe in the kitchen. Her Mom and Dad taught her how to use the stove and oven. She learned how important it was to use pot holders. She always asked for help when she needed it.

When Katie was ten, her favorite game was restaurant. When her brothers and sister had friends over, she would make up names for her restaurant, like "Katie's Cafe." She also designed pretty menus that listed all their favorite things to eat. She would set the table with placemats and napkins. Katie always told her "guests" to mind their manners, because this was a very fancy restaurant.

Her menu looked like this:

> ≫♥≪ Katie's Cafe ≫♥≪
>
> Appetizer: Katie's famous taco dip
>   served with taco chips
> Salad: Katie's fresh garden salad
>   with ranch dressing
> Entree: Katie's peanut butter and
>   jelly sandwiches
> Dessert: Katie's yummy cherry
>   delight

She would write her guests' orders on a note pad. Then she would prepare their meals. All the friends were very impressed at how yummy her food tasted.

Katie also discovered that meals need to be well balanced. Her menu included the food groups: meat, vegetables, fruit, bread and dairy products. She always served milk to her guests; and sometimes made them chocolate milk when they were celebrating a special occasion.

Katie's guests enjoyed the time they spent dining at Katie's Cafe. They always asked when they could come again.

CHAPTER THREE

Holiday Traditions

3

Katie's favorite time of year was the holiday season. She couldn't wait to start cooking her family's favorites.

For Katie, the holiday season started the day after Thanksgiving. Katie asked her Mom, "Can we make our holiday coffee cakes today?" And then she thought a few minutes about the old recipe card that Mom always got down from the shelf and asked, "Mom, we have made the same coffee cakes my entire life, where did the recipe come from?"

Katie's Mom answered, "My grandmother made them when I was a little girl. She would be your great-grandmother." Mom smiled and added, "I wish you could have met her; she made every occasion very special. Traditions are a big part of what makes each family special. We can always add to our traditions any time you think of something that the family would enjoy."

Katie thought about how much fun her family traditions were and wanted to add one of her own. As they were planning the holiday meal, Mom said, "What would you like to have for dinner this year?"

Katie was sitting at the kitchen table, looking outside at the pretty snow falling on the ground when an idea popped into her head. She was watching her brother and sister outside playing in the snow, making the first snowman of the season.

"Mom, could I make the mashed potatoes this year? I have a wonderful idea," said Katie. She was going to make the mashed potatoes into snowmen and decorate them.

She first made the mashed potatoes and placed them in a pastry bag. With the pastry bag she made three balls that made the snowmen look as if they were lying down. She used raisins for the eyes, cheese cubes for the buttons, a carrot piece for the nose, and the mouth was made of apple peel. They were beautiful.

Her brothers, sister, and cousins loved her snowmen potatoes and they tasted great. Mom said, "A successful chef is always creative." It was the most festive holiday dinner her family had ever known ... and the start of a new tradition.

CHAPTER FOUR

School Project

4

When Katie was in the fourth grade, a guest speaker came to her class. The speaker talked about careers.

She asked each of the children what they wanted to be when they grew up. She said, "It is very important to do something you love, because then you'll take pride in your job and perform it the best you can."

Katie and her friends had fun talking about the different things they liked to do.

Lizzy loved to play with her dolls and she spent many hours in her free time with them. Lizzy and her Mom had designed and constructed her own doll house. She loved rearranging the furniture and decorating the house for the different holidays.

Emily liked science and performing experiments in science class. She received a chemistry set for Christmas that year and enjoyed experimenting and looking at slides under the microscope. Emily's favorite part of school was entering the science fair each year.

Lindsey had fun playing office. She pretended she was on the phone making appointments and arranging meetings. She worked on her computer every chance she could.

After their discussion, the speaker asked them to take out a piece of paper and list all the things they liked to do. Katie wrote:

● WHAT I LIKE TO DO:

1. Cook with my dad
2. Go shopping
3. Go out to dinner
4. Make things pretty
5. Play with friends

The guest speaker then said, "Now, list as many different jobs as you can think of around our town that sound like they might be fun to do." They each made up a list. The speaker reminded them, "You might list jobs your parents or people you know have."

Katie's class listed over twenty careers, including owning your own business, doctor, secretary, salesperson, architect, lawyer, and on and on.

Katie knew exactly what she would like to do, "I would like to own my own restaurant. I could be the head chef. My restaurant would be very fancy and serve wonderful food. Everyone in my town would love to come there."

The speaker said, "Your assignment for tonight is to write a research paper on your chosen career. You should include what kind of schooling is required, and what type of experience you will need to succeed in your career."

She told them that their research could include interviewing a person who held that job currently, going to the library, and even finding out what they needed to start their business.

Katie went home to begin her research. She decided she needed lots of help. She went to the library and checked out books on business, restaurants, and chefs. Katie learned that she must be very good in math, reading, and science if she was going to be a chef and own her own restaurant.

Katie had to make sure her math was good so she would know how much to charge for her meals, give the correct change back to her customers, and increase the amount of ingredients in a recipe. She thought combining just the right spices was like a chemistry experiment! Reading was important to ensure she was putting all the right ingredients in her famous recipes.

When Katie thought of all she needed to learn she decided to ask the chef at the best restaurant in town where he went to school and what he learned there. His name was Tony.

Tony said, "I went to college and completed classes in business, restaurant management, and nutrition. After I graduated from college, I went to the Cooking Academy." He said, "It is the best cooking school around."

Tony explained how he learned to make all types of special foods from all over the world. The Cooking Academy taught him how to make appetizers, salads, main courses and, of course, yummy desserts.

Katie asked him, "Did you learn how to make Oysters Rockefeller in cooking school?"

Chef Tony said, "Of course I did."

Katie told him, "Oysters have always been my favorite food."

Katie thanked Chef Tony for sharing the information with her and went home to work on her research paper. She had her books and notes open on her desk. She was so excited about what she had already learned. It had been a busy day for her already. She thought, I'm so tired, I'll lay my head down on my desk for just a minute and organize my thoughts. She fell asleep ... and started to dream ... zzzzzzzz.

CHAPTER FIVE

Katie's Dream

5

Katie's alarm clock woke her up early in the morning. She had a very busy day scheduled; her new restaurant was opening soon. She had many tasks to complete and people to meet. This was the day she had dreamed of since she was in fourth grade.

First, she had to meet with her architect, Lizzy. Lizzy had designed Katie's Cafe. They spent many hours together planning what the restaurant would look like. They had decided on a very pretty and elegant look. Lizzy had helped her choose the color scheme, and most importantly the floor plan of the dining room. The biggest decision was how many people she wanted to seat for dinner. They needed a waiting area, a coat room, restrooms, and a very big kitchen.

Then she had a meeting with her lawyer, Morgan, to make sure the lease on the building was correct and the papers were signed. Morgan also made sure she had business needs met like insurance, taxes, and utilities. Katie was almost ready to open.

Katie was the head chef, and her specialty was French cooking. She hired lots of people to make sure her restaurant ran smoothly. These included waitresses, bus people, extra cooks, dishwashers, and, of course, a maitre d'.

She held a staff meeting so everyone would get to know each other. Katie thought, "I'm glad I took business management classes in college. It really helps me to know how to run this restaurant."

Katie made sure that everyone who worked for her knew that her goal was to give very special attention to every customer so they would want to come back again and again.

Next on the agenda was shopping. Katie needed to buy lots of pots and pans, and cooking utensils. Her

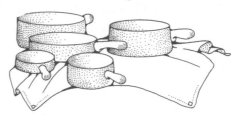

dishes were hand made by her friend Maggie, who owned a pottery shop. The plates had the Katie's Cafe logo on them and they matched the colors that Lizzy had selected for the restaurant. They were very pretty.

Her next stop was the seafood and vegetable markets. She wanted to have all her fruits and vegetables fresh and, of course, have the very best oysters. Oysters Rockefeller was still her specialty. She knew most people would order them and she did not want to run out.

Her next meeting was with her fashion designer Cayley. Katie asked Cayley to design the waitress outfits. Cayley was an excellent seamstress. She had all the uniforms ready when Katie arrived. With her errands complete, and the cafe looking exceptionally beautiful, she was ready to open.

Katie spent her opening day in the restaurant taking reservations and preparing her famous sauces. Five o'clock came very quickly, and she was ready to serve her first customer.

The television station and newspaper reporters were all there to talk and write about the new restaurant in town named Katie's Cafe.

Katie opened her doors and the tables filled quickly. The town was very excited to have a new gourmet restaurant opening.

Katie greeted her customers at the door. She was so excited that many of her friends were there to offer their support. She also checked on her customers after their meal was served to make sure everything was perfect. Then she would make her way back to the kitchen to prepare her next order. Luckily, she had hired extra cooks to prepare the salads and desserts.

At eleven o'clock that evening her restaurant closed. She sat down to rest after her long day and thought, "I have made my dream come true." She was most thankful that her Dad had been her first customer, since he had always been her inspiration ...

CHAPTER SIX

Back To Work

6

Katie woke up and looked at the clock; it was already seven o'clock. She said, "I must have fallen asleep, but, I had the most exciting dream. I'd better start my research paper." She knew it would be easy because she knew now what it took to manage a restaurant.

When she was finished she knew that being a chef was the career she wanted. She would study hard in school and continue to cook and to create recipes of her own.

When she finished with college and the Cooking Academy she could open Katie's Cafe ... the best restaurant in town. She knew it would be hard work, but it was her dream and she was going to make it happen.

THE END

7

Be A Chef

ACTIVITIES:

1. DESIGN YOUR OWN
   RECIPE CARDS

2. HOW TO PROPERLY
   SET YOUR TABLE

3. KATIE'S FAMOUS
   RECIPES

Activity One

DESIGN YOUR OWN RECIPE CARDS

A. Start with a blank index card.

Recipe for: _____
From: Chef Katie   Serves: _____
Ingredients: _____
_____
_____
_____
Directions: _____
_____
_____ ❥♥❦ Enjoy! ❥♥❦ _____
_____

B. Example above:
- Name of recipe
- Name of chef (your name) and how many people the recipe serves
- Ingredients:
- Directions:
- Decorate the recipe card

C. Give your favorite recipes to friends

Bon Appétit!

Activity Two
How To Properly Set Your Table

Setting a beautiful table for your formal dinners is fun. The rules never change. What you learn at age ten will still hold true at age fifty. Setting a proper table will always impress your guest.

First, start with a pretty tablecloth or placemat and napkins. Decorate the center of your table with holiday decorations, flowers, or candles. Ask your mom if you can use the good china and glasses. Be creative!

- Forks are always placed to the left of the plate; knives and spoons are placed to the right.
- Place silverware in the order in which you will use it, always placing the first silverware to be used farthest from the plate.
- The table above is set for a five course meal: fruit appetizer, soup, salad, main course, and dessert, plus bread & butter, and beverage. The courses are served in order with their own silverware. They are labeled above.

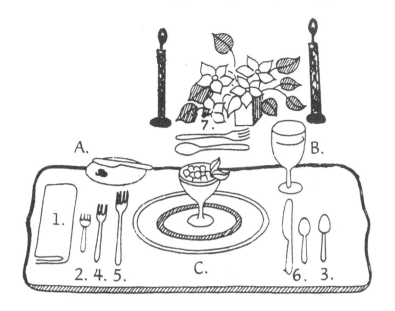

- The bread and butter plate is placed to the upper left of the forks, the beverage glass is placed above the knives and spoons.
- The order in which you use the silverware is labeled on the drawing:

7. Dessert fork or spoon

A. Bread & butter plate and knife   B. Beverage Glass

1. Napkin (place on your lap)
                              C. Plate
2. Appetizer fork   6. Main course
                                               knife & spoon
4. Salad fork   3. Soup spoon
5. Main course fork

HAPPY ENTERTAINING AND BON APPÉTIT

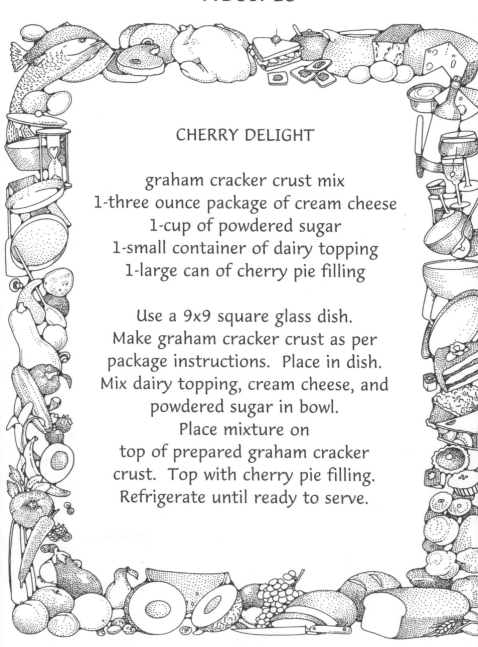

Activity Three
KATIE'S FAMOUS
RECIPES

CHERRY DELIGHT

graham cracker crust mix
1-three ounce package of cream cheese
1-cup of powdered sugar
1-small container of dairy topping
1-large can of cherry pie filling

Use a 9x9 square glass dish.
Make graham cracker crust as per
package instructions. Place in dish.
Mix dairy topping, cream cheese, and
powdered sugar in bowl.
Place mixture on
top of prepared graham cracker
crust. Top with cherry pie filling.
Refrigerate until ready to serve.

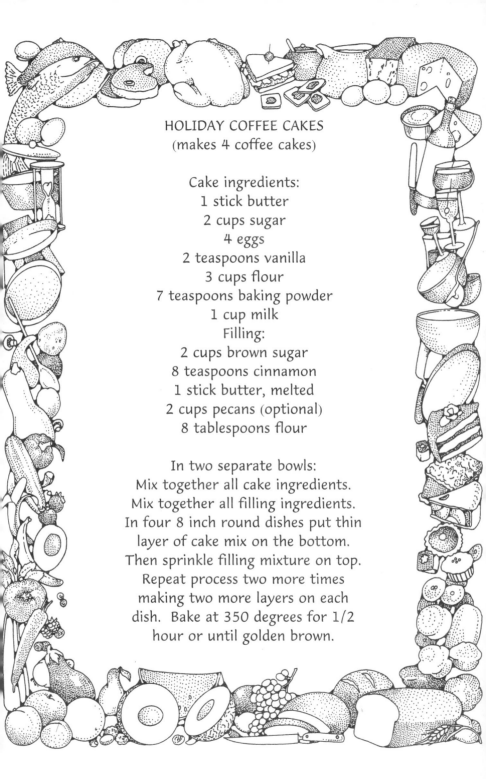

HOLIDAY COFFEE CAKES
(makes 4 coffee cakes)

Cake ingredients:
1 stick butter
2 cups sugar
4 eggs
2 teaspoons vanilla
3 cups flour
7 teaspoons baking powder
1 cup milk
Filling:
2 cups brown sugar
8 teaspoons cinnamon
1 stick butter, melted
2 cups pecans (optional)
8 tablespoons flour

In two separate bowls:
Mix together all cake ingredients.
Mix together all filling ingredients.
In four 8 inch round dishes put thin
layer of cake mix on the bottom.
Then sprinkle filling mixture on top.
Repeat process two more times
making two more layers on each
dish. Bake at 350 degrees for 1/2
hour or until golden brown.

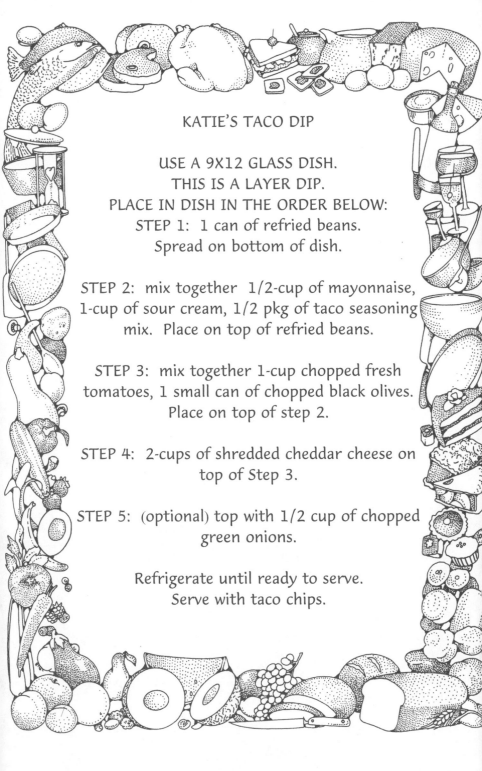

KATIE'S TACO DIP

USE A 9X12 GLASS DISH.
THIS IS A LAYER DIP.
PLACE IN DISH IN THE ORDER BELOW:
STEP 1: 1 can of refried beans.
Spread on bottom of dish.

STEP 2: mix together 1/2-cup of mayonnaise,
1-cup of sour cream, 1/2 pkg of taco seasoning
mix. Place on top of refried beans.

STEP 3: mix together 1-cup chopped fresh
tomatoes, 1 small can of chopped black olives.
Place on top of step 2.

STEP 4: 2-cups of shredded cheddar cheese on
top of Step 3.

STEP 5: (optional) top with 1/2 cup of chopped
green onions.

Refrigerate until ready to serve.
Serve with taco chips.

FESTIVE SNOWMAN POTATOES

Peel skins off 3 lbs of potatoes.
Boil until tender.
Mash thoroughly while adding
milk and butter until smooth.

Place mashed potatoes into pastry bag
Squeeze out circles in three sizes
onto greased cookie sheet.

Decorate snowman with eyes,
nose, mouth, and buttons.
Be creative.

Bake in oven at 350 degrees
for 10 minutes.
Serve immediately. Use spatula to
remove snowman from cookie sheet.

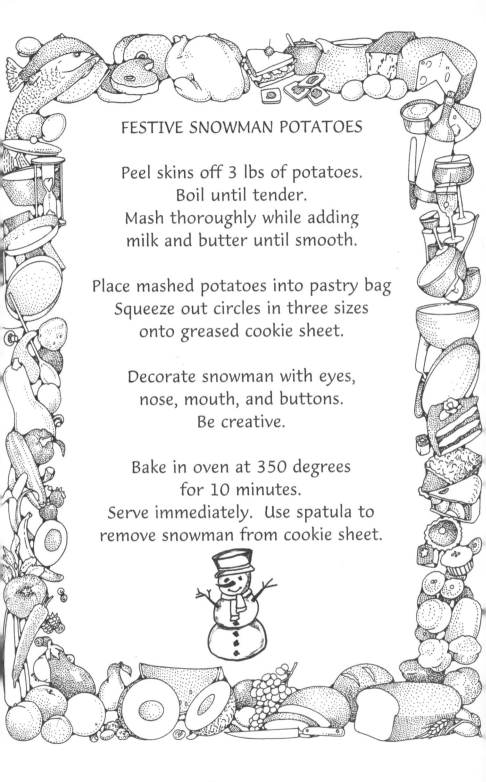

KATIE'S OYSTERS ROCKEFELLER

Serves 4

3 green onions (white part and 1 inch
green part), minced
1 rib of celery, diced
1 tablespoon butter
1 cup chopped fresh spinach
1 tablespoon fine dry bread crumbs
1/4 pound of butter, softened
2 strips bacon, fried crisp, then crumbled
salt to taste
12 fresh oysters on the half shell

Preheat oven to 450°F. Saute onions and celery in 1 Tbl. butter until tender. Add chopped spinach and cook one minute; remove from heat. Add bread crumbs and salt. Blend together with the softened 1/4 lb. butter and bacon.

In a shallow baking pan (large enough to hold all the oysters) arrange oysters on their shells in a pan and top each with about 1 teaspoon of the saute mix.
Bake 10 minutes until hot and bubbly.
Serve at once.
Enjoy!

Hint:
Katie likes to chop her oysters into bite size pieces and place in the half shells before topping.

8
Vocabulary

<u>Appetizer:</u> food that whets the appetite; small meal eaten before the main course.

<u>Architect:</u> a person who graduates from an architecture school, specializing in designing buildings and structures.

<u>Bon Appétit:</u> a phrase which means happy eating.

<u>Career:</u> a specific occupation or job a person does during his or her lifetime.

<u>Chef:</u> the head cook of a restaurant.

<u>Chemistry:</u> The science that studies chemical properties of changes using experiments.

<u>Decorate:</u> to make something more beautiful.

<u>Doctor:</u> a person who has graduated from a medical school.

<u>Entree:</u> the main course of a meal.

<u>Fashion Designer:</u> a person who creates any type of clothing.

<u>Festive:</u> pertaining to becoming a feast or a joyous celebration.

<u>Gourmet:</u> a meal that is considered fine or special.

<u>Interior Designer:</u> a person who makes interiors of buildings beautiful and functional.

<u>Ingredients:</u> that which makes up a recipe, i.e., spices, meats, fruits, vegetables, etc.

<u>Insurance:</u> that which you buy to protect a person or business against certain risk, i.e., fire, injury, etc.

<u>Lawyer:</u> a person who graduates from law school who writes contracts and practices the law.

<u>Maitre d':</u> a head waiter in a fine restaurant.

<u>Tradition:</u> The practice of passing down customs or beliefs from parents to children.